I0452180

CHRISTMAS EVE

A Sweet Christmas Volume 2

SAMANTHA JACOBEY

Lavish
Publishing LLC

This book is a work of fiction. The characters, incidents, and dialogue are drawn from the author's imagination and are not to be construed as real. Any resemblance to actual events or persons, living or dead, is entirely coincidental.

CHRISTMAS EVE. Copyright 2016 ©

All rights reserved under International and Pan-American Copyright Conventions. By payment of the required fees, you have been granted the non-exclusive, non-transferable right to access and read the text of this e-book on-screen. No part of this text may be reproduced, transmitted, down-loaded, decompiled, reverse engineered, or stored in or introduced into any information storage and retrieval system, in any form or by any means, whether electronic or mechanical, now known or hereinafter invented, without the express written permission of Lavish Publishing, LLC.

First Edition

A Sweet Christmas Series book 2

2016 Lavish Publishing, LLC

All Rights Reserved

Published in the United States by Lavish Publishing, LLC, Midland, TX

Cover Design by: WYCKED INK

Cover Images: ADOBE STOCK

Paperback edition

ISBN: 9781944985165

www.LavishPublishing.com

Contents

Prologue

CANDY JOGGED in place while glaring at the light on a corner a few blocks from the giant old house she shared with Gary, her mother, and her son. Glancing at the device on her wrist, she noted her pulse and calories burned with a small grin. *Right on target,* she mused. She had been making the same run every morning for months and had a net loss of over forty pounds to show for it. *Well, between the running and my diet.* She smiled more broadly as she crossed the quiet street.

Her breath frosting and tingling her nostrils, she thought about the first day she had made the trip, only she hadn't run that morning. It had been more like a brisk walk and not intended to be exercise at all. She had needed to clear her head and get some things straight, at least for herself. Things that were getting the better of her no matter how hard she fought them. Feeling nostalgic, she retraced her past; each time her foot hit the ground, another memory jarred loose and was forced to the surface for evaluation.

Candy had met Gerald Ford over a year ago while working in a convenience store. The night shift supervisor at the firehouse a few streets from the shop, he came in often for a pack of cigarettes and a bit of friendly banter. She couldn't recall exactly when it had happened, but the anniversary of his first request for a date was at hand, and the idea of it pulled her thoughts deeper into the past.

Candy hadn't dated much before Gary. Well, any at all if she were honest about it. Her father had been killed in the line of duty when she was only ten, and following that one, sad event, her life had marched along, one horrific circumstance after another.

Her mother had become an alcoholic, and Candice herself had been drawn in by a group of boys who only used her. Wanting to fit in and make friends, she had allowed their games to escalate, and her son, Dakota, had been the result. A long story and one the girl avoided telling even to herself, she scowled at the dark cloud of conditions surrounding her only child's conception and birth.

Her thoughts in turmoil, Candice's feet hit the ground faster, and her arms pumped as she sped down the walk, as if the ghosts of her past had picked up her scent and made pursuit. Arriving at the next light, she gulped in air as her heart pounded inside her chest. Swallowing, she fumbled with her water bottle and glared at the glowing red indicator. Focusing on the symbol to stop, she forced her breathing down and muttered, "Get off it. You can't change what happened."

Moving forward to last Christmas and the fire, with Gary's saving her son and mother, she recalled she had changed more than just physically over the last year. Emotionally, she had arrived at a better place even as she had fought the progress tooth and nail. He had taken the family into his home. Given them shelter, friendship, and love. It had been hard for her to accept, but by the time he had gotten his promotion to fire investigator, she had been ready for a real relationship—ready to date him and to face what lay before them.

Calmer when the light cycled, Candy resumed her easy jog. Becoming her best friend, she had learned to trust Gary with her past, present, and future. It had not been an easy road. He had shown a great deal of patience on more than one occasion, and her gratitude, though always present, was often buried under layers of anger and fear.

Making the last turn, Candy smiled again as she approached the large house she had come to call home Tomorrow night, they would be hosting a Halloween party for a few family and friends. An anxious feeling twisted her gut, knowing the huge surprise the couple had in store for their unsuspecting guests. Her life had been crazy for years, but if things worked out as she and Gary hoped, it was about to calm down.

The idea of being normal, of having what everyone else has, appealed to her. Gerald Ford had become so much more than some guy buying smokes and making small talk. More than a friend but not yet a lover. "It'll come," she whispered to herself as she climbed the steps. "Have a little faith that dreams really do come true." She sighed as she twisted the handle and made her way inside.

ONE

Party Surprise

"MOM, ARE YOU IN HERE?" Candy called as she crossed the kitchen. Her mother had been given the servant's suite in Gary's enormous house when they moved in—a small sitting area, bed and bath, perfect for allowing her privacy while keeping her under their roof and out of a nursing home. Entering with a soft knock, she noticed that the screen door lay open, and a cool draft blew in from her mother's private entrance to the back porch. "Mom, you know Gary likes to keep the bills down. Why is your door standing open again?"

"Gary doesn't mind the bills," her mother replied as Candy joined her on the back veranda. "We're positioning the jack-o-lanterns." Lanelle indicated the boy stooped over and pushing against an over-sized pumpkin.

"Still," Candy insisted, "please close the doors when you go out. No sense in wasting the heat."

Laneile sighed at how much her daughter sounded

like an old fuddy-duddy. "Smile and don't worry so much," she instructed her only child.

Candice grimaced at her response. She had been trying to do precisely that, but old habits were hard to break. She had spent years perfecting her Debbie-Downer persona, and it would take a great deal of practice to let her go completely. "I think everything inside is set," she replied as she knelt beside her son. "You need some help, baby?"

"Punkins," Dakota replied, smiling at her in his typical happy manner.

"Yes, pumpkins." She grinned in earnest. "They look great, baby," she lied as they adjusted the gutted gourd. Lighting the candle for him, it shown brightly through the hole of his attempt at a smiling face.

Gary had picked up half a dozen pumpkins for them to carve a few days before, and she had enjoyed watching the pair of them clean out the gunk and create the "faces" with varying degrees of success. The best ones had been placed on the front side of the house, where their guests would enter through the main entrance.

"We need to get ready for the party, hun," she cajoled.

"Party." He stood abruptly, turning to his grandmother. "Party, Mimi."

"Yes, we have to get washed and ready," Lanelle agreed, taking his hand and leading him inside to her lavatory.

Candy remained behind, watching after the pair. Her mother had been with Dakota his entire life, and she hated to think how hard it would be on him if, or when, they lost her. Her mother's health had not been stellar since her stroke two years ago, and her recovery after the fire had been difficult. Refusing to fall into the black abyss of "what if," Candy went inside, closing the wooden cover firmly behind her. "I'll take him, Mom," she announced. "You get yourself ready, and we'll see you in the living room in half an hour."

Seizing Daks' hand, she led him into the kitchen and then up the stairs. "Are you excited, baby?"

Dakota pulled free, making a haphazard dash for the bedroom that had become his. Across the hall from Gary's room, a full-sized bathroom connected it to the one his mother occupied. Inside, he flung open his closet and grasped eagerly at his fireman costume.

Swallowing the lump in her throat, Candy helped him place his feet into the pants and pull them into place over his jeans. "Easy, baby," she instructed as they worked the top onto his wriggling body and snapped the realistic-looking clasps. "Don't forget your ax," she said more cheerily than she felt as she handed him the plastic replica. It still bothered her that he loved firemen so much even though he would never be one. His limitations would never allow it.

Gurgling through his teeth, the boy's happiness remained clear. Giving the tool a wave in the air, he cackled out loud before he limped towards the door to descend the old wooden stairs.

"Hold on to the railing," his mother called after

him before she used the bathroom to access her own room.

Running a brush through her long honey-brown locks, she sighed anxiously. Gary's mother and father would be arriving later, having a previous engagement to attend, but a few of their guests would be there shortly, and she needed to be ready to play hostess when they arrived.

Clomping down after her son a few minutes later, Candy inhaled deeply through her mouth, then forced the air out slowly through her nostrils in an effort to relax. The scent of Gary's cooking filled the house, but it had been days since she felt hungry.

Although the sun had only begun to set, she flicked on the porch light and stared out the front glass at the street and the vehicle that had stopped short of the drive. One of Gary's cousins, his wife, and their two sons exited the SUV and made their way up the walk.

"Are you nervous?" Gary asked as his hands gave her shoulders a squeeze. Leaning over her, his palms slid down her arms affectionately as he nuzzled her ear as he tenderly drew her close.

"No." She smiled up at him. "I'm ready. Get the door?" she asked as the bell chimed.

Grinning, he turned to let the first arrivals in and announced, "Boys, Daks has the games ready to go in the den. I think you know the way." He raised a hand to indicate the hall that would take them to the family room. "But don't start the movie until you get back," he instructed.

The family pack of youngsters would be taking the boy out for a small trip around the block for a bit of trick-or-treating after dinner. He smiled at the thought of Dakota behaving like an ordinary child, something he and Candy had been working on since they met. They had even located a special private school for him, which she had reluctantly allowed him to pay for. Every small victory mattered. Dakota might never be "normal," but he would get every opportunity to at least try if Gary could help it.

"Hello, Gary." Robert extended a hand.

Giving him a firm shake, Gerald grinned deviously. He knew their surprise had Candy on edge, but he couldn't wait to make their announcement. "Dinner is in the dining room. We'll eat as soon as Mom and Dad arrive."

"Wonderful." Paula removed her jacket and offered it to him. "Candy, as lovely as ever." The slender woman admired the petite brunette's emerging figure beneath her fitted gown. "How much weight have you lost?"

"Forty-three pounds," Candy admitted with a flush. "It feels good, too."

"I'm sure it does." Paula leaned in for a small hug before moving past her and allowing more guests to enter the large living room that occupied the majority of the ground floor.

Half an hour later, Gary's parents made their entrance, and everyone moved to the dining room, where the adults would be enjoying dinner. The eight children would remain in the kitchen and had already been served. The two eldest of them would take the troop out for their evening of begging the neighbors for treats as soon as they had eaten, and Candy could feel her hands trembling as she reached to serve her plate.

"Dammit," she muttered under her breath as she forced her fingers to work. Leaning across the table, she spooned a helping of potatoes. Eveline's glare stopped her in mid-motion, and she returned the large serving spoon to the bowl and sat down.

"Would you like some bread?" the older woman asked pointedly as she lifted a basket and began passing it around from left to right.

Crap, I forgot, Candy thought to herself. Gary's family was different than she had been raised, and mealtimes still served as a reminder; she wasn't one of them.

"You ok?" Gary whispered next to her as she settled back into her seat.

"Yes." She nodded, accepting a serving dish from him. "I'm still not used to the way you guys treat dinner like a formal affair," she admitted quietly. A few of those closest to her snickered at her observation, as their dining customs came as second nature to them.

Pouring herself a generous glass of wine, Eveline raised the glass to the girl across the table from her and then sipped from it silently. Eve had an ominous feeling about spending the evening with the girl she hadn't been able to get rid of and consoled herself the best she could. She felt confident that her only son,

Gary, could do worse than Candice Parker, but she had certainly hoped for much better than the girl across from her and all her baggage.

Candy swallowed her anxiety and remembered to smile as she served her plate and passed each dish. Her mother seated on her right, she helped her with the heavier ones. Each bowl that passed only added to her discomfort. She knew that many things in her life had changed in the last year and more than just eating out of serving bowls rather than saucepans. Gary had become a fixture in her world, a staple that she lived on, and she could not deny that she had become happy with him despite her early protests.

However, she got the distinct impression that his family was only polite to her out of courtesy. On more than one occasion, she had felt as if they were not welcome by his mother and cousins, and it had left a sour taste in her mouth. *Just breathe,* she reminded herself silently. *After dinner, Cathy and some of my other friends will show up, and things will be a lot less stuffy around here.*

A year ago, Candy had no friends to speak of, but since she had signed up for school last spring, she had made a few, with Cathy being the closest friendship she had forged in years. Getting her GED this past summer, she had started at the junior college the month before. *Only the local school and not a fancy university, but still.* She smiled to herself. She had been working to better herself and her life, physically and mentally, and that's what mattered.

"Dinner is delicious, baby," she complimented Gary openly.

"Thanks, kitten." He smiled shyly, only cutting his mother a quick glance.

"Candice did not prepare the meal?" Eve asked in a sharp tone.

"No," the girl volunteered happily. "Oh, I can cook, but why should I when Gary is so much better at it?"

The chairs creaked as their guests shifted nervously for a moment. Then Gary's father seemed to come to her rescue. "We all have our talents," he stated as he raised his glass to his son while earning a dark glare from his wife.

Clearing her throat and patting her napkin to her lips, Candy glanced around at the gathering, her mind drifting back to the first time she had met Gary's family. They had been living in his house since the fire had destroyed their apartment, and the four of them—Candy, Lanelle, Dakota, and Gary—had settled into a routine. She still had not agreed to date him, but they had become comfortable, nonetheless.

On the evening of that first meeting, she had been the one to prepare the meal, and she could still see the disgusted look on Eveline's face when she placed her assortment of pots and pans on the table before her. The older woman had said nothing, but Candy could tell from the start that she wasn't measuring up to her expectations.

Later that night, she had overheard the woman tell her son as they prepared to leave, "*I hope you haven't settled on this one. I mean, it's generous of you to help them, but they are not the family for you, Gary."*

Candy herself had told him as much after the fire destroyed their home and she had reluctantly moved in with him. However, she had gotten past that. To know his mother felt the same way and had told him so had been a hard blow.

The words had stung, and Candy's eyes grew misty for a moment, despite her sitting across from Eve as she recalled them. She had remembered them often, and they came to her every time she thought about what their future might hold. *They are not the family for you, Gary.* Forcing herself to eat the delicious food, she wondered how the evening would end —how Eveline would react to their coming surprise.

An hour later, the table had been cleared, and the group gathered in the large living area. Candy's few friends had arrived, and music filled the air as everyone lingered, sitting, standing, and enjoying the evening while the kids made the traditional pass through the neighborhood. It seemed odd to her that they would have a large dinner gathering on Halloween when Thanksgiving and Christmas seemed better suited, but she had learned last year that Gary's parents were snowbirds.

The first week of November, Eve and Roger would be moving to their Florida summer home and would not return until the following spring. This was their family gathering for the season. Anyone who wanted to see them in between would have to make the trip south, and it gave Candy a twinge of guilt that

Gary had failed to make that journey the previous year because of her. Of course, he hadn't said so, but Eve had been sure to point it out when they later met.

Turning off the sound system at the end of the song, Gary announced loudly, "Everyone, can I have your attention, please? Please, gather round." He stepped to the front of the fireplace and waited for Candice to join him.

Her legs like Jello, Candy shuffled past the onlookers who moved aside for her. Taking his hand, she stared up at Gary, strengthened by his resolve. Casting a quick glance at the silver fox she had come to know as his father, an older man who was still quite handsome despite the grey of his hair, she smiled briefly. *Not everyone in his family hates me,* she reassured herself.

"We wanted to thank you all for coming this evening. I know since Aunt Betty's passing, things have changed a lot around here. I'm sure I wasn't the only one surprised that she chose to leave this old place to me, but I have to admit I've come to be quite happy that she did," he stated while smiling down warmly at the girl next to him.

Her heart beating wildly inside her chest, Candy squeezed his hand. *It's ok.* She steadied herself. They had rehearsed for this moment a few days before, but standing there, before his family, she found each breath a struggle. Her lips curled into a large grin, she waited as his fingers smoothed a few hairs out of her face.

Her mind turning, she wondered if he had told

anyone what was coming next. She had been tempted to spill the beans to a couple of her new girlfriends and suspected that both Cathy and her mother were going to be miffed that she didn't share. But in the end, she had managed to remain tight-lipped. As far as she knew, their announcement would be a surprise to them all.

"Candy and I are getting married," he said in a hushed voice. "This Christmas," he stated more firmly. Looking up, his mother's face had paled to ash-white, and he held on to his bride to be. "Now, who's coming to the wedding?" he called jovially.

The noise level in the room grew exponentially as joyous shouts from their friends filled the space, but Candice could see none of his blood relations were celebrating. On the contrary, their pallor had matched that of his mother, and concerned glances and whispers came from them as they gathered in the far corner to discuss the turn of events amongst themselves.

Gary didn't seem to notice their disbelief, or if he did, he chose to ignore it. Instead, he cranked up the stereo and offered Candy his hand. They had been learning to dance together one evening a week for months, and he couldn't wait to show off their skills and celebrate the future he had dreamed of—a life with Candice Parker—and he wasn't about to let his family ruin a single minute of it.

TWO

All the Trimmings

CANDY CLIMBED into the front passenger seat of his Chevy Suburban and waited for Gary to start the engine. Folding her hands in front of her, she rehearsed what she wanted to say, having made a list for when they were seated at their favorite restaurant.

"Relax, sweetness," Gary instructed as he backed down the drive. "Your mom and Dakota will be fine," he teased.

"I'm not worried about them." She sighed loudly. They left Dakota in Lanelle's care regularly, especially when they needed to talk, as deep or heavy conversations were always held in private. "Let's not get into it until we've ordered dinner."

"Ok." He cut her a quick glance, aware that she had been tense since their announcement the evening before. Going over his own list of topics to discuss, he grinned to himself. They were going to have a beautiful wedding with all the trimmings; he would see to that. It had taken him a year to get to this point with the girl of his dreams, and he intended to make the most of it no matter how his mother felt about it.

However, Eveline had called him that morning to inform him that they were canceling their trip to Florida. Shocking news, to say the least. She had not gone so far as to say that they were upset by his decision, but he could tell she would not make things easy for them. The sooner he and Candy had firm plans about their big day, the better.

Arriving at their favorite spot, he parked his SUV and climbed out. Helping her out her side, he laid his hand on her far shoulder and allowed the arm to hang behind her in a lovingly possessive manner. Candy was still not big on displays of affection, but she had been coming around, and he took every opportunity to touch her and draw her closer to him on a physical level.

Once they were in their seats and steaks had been ordered, he lifted his glass of wine and made a toast. "To Candy. The girl I will spend my life with."

"Oh, Gary." The woman across from him flushed prettily. Biting her lip, she hesitated before drinking a sip from her own glass. "We need to talk," she stated firmly.

"Yes, we do," he readily agreed. "We need to decide which day we want to hold the wedding. And are we still on for a small ceremony, or have you decided that you would like a larger function? I mean, a girl only gets married once, and I'll see to it that you get the wedding you've always wanted."

His smile broad, he appeared so pleased. Candy

felt a twinge of guilt at what she had on her list to discuss, as wedding plans had fallen to the bottom. "Gary, let's not get ahead of ourselves, ok? There are a lot of things we need to talk about before we start ordering dresses and cakes with flowers on top."

"A little bride and groom go on top." He chuckled, keeping his tone light. "It's ok, kitten. I know you're scared—"

"I'm not scared," she cut him off. "You saw the look on your mother's face. Your family isn't going to take this marriage lying down." Gary had always portrayed his family as ordinary, but she had growing suspicions that they weren't and that trouble lay ahead.

Heaving a deep sigh, Gary placed his elbows on the table and folded his hands in front of his face. Tapping his knuckles against his lips for a moment, he considered addressing the elephant in the room, then asked in a quiet tone, "Do you really want to marry me?"

Candy's mouth fell open, and she gasped. "Of course I do!"

Relief clearly etched on his rugged features, he leaned eagerly towards her. "Then you need a much thicker skin. You and I are in this together, and we have to stand up to them—together. Tonight, we need to work out what our wedding is going to look like, and we have to stick to that plan and not let anyone talk us into anything different."

"You think that she will try?" Toying with her

napkin, Candy blinked back tears as her voice cracked.

"I'm sure she will." He reached for her hand and squeezed her across the table. "Baby, I love you. And you love me. We can't let anything get in the way of that. Promise me from here on we stick together on this. They can't beat us if we have each other's backs."

"You make it sound as if a fight is coming." She sniffed.

"Well, I hope not." He shrugged. "But knowing my mother, I'm thinking we should be prepared for anything. They canceled their trip to Florida," he informed her calmly.

"Canceled their trip!" She gasped. "They go every year without fail."

"I know." He drew his hand away to refold them in front of his face. "She called to let me know this morning, and that has me worried. We have to be tough, kitten."

"Ok." Candy nodded, her lip forming a small pout. "I still want a small wedding. With a simple dress, and yes, in the living room at the house is perfect. I love it there, in front of the fireplace." She smiled in spite of her inner turmoil. "I do love you, too, Gary. I want this." She had had her misgivings, but when she finally agreed to be his wife, she had meant it.

Gulping a few large swallows of her wine, Candy started at the top of her list. "I need to be sure, though. If your parents were to react, you know, like to disown you or anything like that. I'm not sure I could take it if they did."

"I don't care if they disown me." He smirked, taking her hand again. "I don't need their money, and I certainly don't hang on their approval. If I did, I never would have been a fireman or done half the things I have in my life."

"Ok." Candy nodded, dropping to item number two. "Then we need to talk about Daks. And my mother, for that matter. They are both going to need care for the rest of their lives. I'm a package deal, and I need to be sure you understand that."

"Baby, we already talked about that, and yes, I understand your mother and son are part of the bargain. They are welcome in our house, here or wherever we may go, for as long as we live. Now, what's going on?" He eyed her suspiciously. "Why are you bringing all of this up when this was all settled when you agreed to marry me?"

"I'm scared, Gary." Her lip trembled. "Seeing how your family reacted made me realize…there's a lot they could use against us. Too many things that could go wrong in all of this. I'm not the only one who would lose here. Daks and Mom, their futures also rest on my choices and what happens between us. I mean, we haven't even made love yet. What if we get into bed on our wedding night and you decide I'm not what you're looking for?"

"Oh my God." He coughed a loud laugh as the waiter placed their plates before them. Clearing his throat against his fist, he struggled to regain his composure, then leaned towards her once again. "Candy, listen to me. I have waited for you even longer than I have known you. I'm not pressuring you for the physical. That will come when it's time and we're both ready."

He could see the sadness in her eyes and pushed on. "Baby, when we met, I loved you as you were, and I love you now." He raised his palms to indicate her more slender form. "You have always been beautiful to me, and nothing is going to change that. And I've had my fill of physical relationships. I'm ready for the next level—the one where sex is great, but it isn't everything…not by a long shot."

"What about kids, Gary?" she asked stiffly. "What if Dakota is all we ever have? I've seen how you are with him and your littler cousins. What if you don't ever get to have a family of your own?"

"A family of my own?" He tossed his napkin on the table angrily. "What are you talking about? You and Daks, you are my family. If it's just us, then it's just us. And your mom, too. Candy, what has gotten into you?"

Tears spilling over, Candice dabbed at them with her napkin. Her voice shaky, she smiled and said, "I needed to know where we stand. I'm afraid you're right about your family going to make a fuss about this, and there's too much at stake for us to get married only to have it all fall apart."

"It isn't going to fall apart. We're tough, and together we'll deal with them and anything else that comes our way. Now, can we please talk about our wedding?" He grinned, hoping she would let it go.

Glancing at her untouched meal, Candy gave him a crooked smile, then selected her knife and fork to begin cutting the meat. "You really think it will be any good when we're finally sleeping in the same bed?"

"Oh, baby." He agreed whole-heartedly. "It's going to be amazing. I can't wait to lay you down. I swear." Digging into his meal, he knew it was the truth, and he swore to himself that nothing would stand in the way of his showing her how much he meant it.

THREE

Holiday Cheer

"MADAM FORD," a young male clerk greeted them as soon as they entered the boutique.

"Hello, Cedric," Eveline replied coolly. "Are our gowns ready for viewing?"

"Yes, ma'am." He turned and indicated a curtain to a private area. "Right this way."

Candy followed the pair, her mouth open in awe. Hanging around the shop were the most extraordinary dresses she had ever seen. A variety of colors and styles, some were obviously wedding gowns, while others were formals for any manner of occasions.

Inside the smaller chamber, a row of seats awaited them. Indicating one, Eve instructed, "Have a seat, dear."

The girl cringed at the affectionate term but obeyed. Her future mother-in-law had called her the night before to arrange their little outing, to which she had reluctantly agreed. They had flown into New York that morning and had checked into a luxury hotel before making their way to their appointment by limo. During that time, Eve had called her dear, sweetheart, or some other condescending nicety at least twenty times, and every single one of them had set Candy's nerves on edge.

Sinking down into the seat, the girl stared at the stage and waited while Eveline gave instructions to their attendant. Then, taking the chair next to her charge, she sat up straight and said firmly, "These will be our selections. Your dress should be elegant and befitting a princess. Gary deserves as much."

Gripping the cushioned armrests, Candy waited, unsure how to respond to such a statement. A moment later, a young woman stepped out onto the short stage to present herself for viewing. Turning slowly, she smiled broadly as she struck various poses.

"That's a bit...poofy...don't you think?" Candy asked in a timid voice, wishing she could be dress shopping with Cathy instead.

"Perhaps you're right," Eve agreed, her fingers resting against her chin as she studied their first option. "Next!" she called loudly while dismissing the current model with a wave of her hand.

The second gown a tightly fitted version, it hung to the tops of the model's toes on the front edge and scraped the floor the rest of the way around, followed by a long train.

"Wow," Candy breathed. "There's no way I could walk in that! It's way too long."

"Don't be silly," Eveline chided. "These are

examples. Whatever we choose will be custom made to fit you."

"Custom made!" Candy gasped. "Won't that be expensive? And are you sure it will be ready in time for the ceremony?"

"We're moving your date to April third," Eve informed her crisply. "Do you like this one? It will be ready in plenty of time, I'm sure."

Her gaze shifting from the dazzling white gown to the woman seated next to her, Candy bit angrily, "Moving our date? You can't just reschedule our wedding!"

"I'm afraid it can't be helped." Eve waved at the slender young lady before them. "Next!"

Leaping to her feet, Candy glowered down at her. "I said—"

"I know what you said." Eve also stood to lean over her, imposing her will with her rigid form. "I've already spoken to Gary about it. Your guest list is appallingly short, and there is no way a single room in that house will accommodate the number of people who will need an invitation. I've booked a cathedral and ballroom here in New York for the first week in April, and it will have to do."

Struck speechless, Candy's face flushed a bright angry red. Clenching her hands into fists at her sides, her teeth ground against each other. Her lips curling, she managed, "You can't do this!"

"I'm afraid that I can." Eveline indicated her chair with an open palm. "Have a seat, Candice. We have six more gowns to view, and then you will choose one. After that, you will need to be measured. From here, we visit the caterer and the baker to order your cake." Placing her hands on her hips, the older woman waited for her orders to be obeyed.

Warm, wet tears streaked down her cheeks as Candy sat down. She wanted to argue, to scream that this was wrong. This was not what she and Gary had decided at all. But how could she? In the middle of a public place, no that wouldn't do at all. *When we get back in the car or at the hotel,* she consoled. *I'll set the record straight.*

Choosing the simplest of the dresses, Candy allowed them to poke and prod her as measurements were taken and arrangements made. The gown would be handmade and take ninety days to deliver, well after their intended nuptials on December twentieth. Oscillating between seething anger and overwhelming grief, she climbed back into the limo that had delivered them to the location.

"Eveline, this is as far as I go," she bit as the door shut behind them.

"Nonsense, child." Eve adjusted herself into the seat. "You wish to marry my son, you must be prepared to take your place within our family. There are certain expectations that must be met, and the proper ceremony is the first step. Gary's father has allowed him too much freedom. It's time that he took his place within the family business, a respectable profession, and left this silly fireman nonsense behind."

Candy stared at her in disbelief. Meddling with

their wedding was one thing, but insinuating that it would encompass other aspects of their lives was more than she could take. "You wouldn't dare! Gary loves his job!" And she did too, now that he was an investigator and not on the front lines.

"We'll see about that." Eve glared out the window, refusing to meet her gaze. "Mark my words. We will make sure our family name and honor are upheld, starting with this wedding. If you can't deal with that, you are free to go any time." She cut her mahogany orbs over at Candy with an icy glare, challenging her to say anymore. When the girl remained silent, she continued, "The next stop is the caterer. We will need a buffet that will feed at least two hundred and fifty guests."

"Two hundred and fifty," Candy echoed breathlessly.

Too stunned to argue, she wondered for a moment what Gary would say when he heard about all of this or if he had secretly agreed to it without consulting her. He had, after all, been the one to tell her she would be picking out her dress with his mother. Maybe he had condoned all the changes.

Tightening her jaw, she resisted the urge to call him at that moment. Instead, she pictured the conversation they would have as soon as she could speak to him in person, which strengthened her resolve to finish the trip without escalating tension with the older woman.

Taking in the next two places, Candy allowed her future relation to select the menu and choose the wedding cake to suit her. She had resigned herself that they would get to the bottom of things as soon as they returned home and fretting about it at the moment was of little use. Besides, if Eve wanted to waste her money on making the arrangements, that was fine by her, even if she had no intention of living up to her end of whatever bargain Eve thought they had.

FOUR

All the Gold

GARY GRIPPED the steering wheel tightly as he drove home from the office. He had been livid to discover that his mother had taken Candy to New York after he had agreed to have her purchase the wedding gown. He had thought a local shop would or should have sufficed.

"Son of a bitch," he cursed under his breath while stopped at a light, his fist slamming down hard enough to bruise his hand. His fiancée would be home waiting for him, and he felt fairly certain that this would be one conversation that wouldn't wait for relocating to their favorite restaurant.

Nope, not this time. He didn't know yet what all his mother had pulled, but he had no doubt that Candy would clue him in as soon as he walked through the door. What's worse, he would have some explaining to do. Drawing a deep breath, he let it out slowly and leaned against the glass with his left elbow. "Women," he spoke aloud to himself in disgust.

Parked in the garage a few minutes later, he frowned at the dark clouds that hung in the sky above. Adjusting his coat against the strong north wind, he had a sneaking suspicion that cold weather loomed in his near future.

Arriving at the back steps, the door opened as he started to climb, and his heart skipped a beat at the sight of Candy's tear-stained face. "Aw, honey. What happened?" he offered, dropping his arms around her and pulling her into a hug.

"Your mother is a real witch. That's what happened," she sniveled. "Did you know she changed the date of our wedding?" Not waiting for a reply, her questions continued in rapid-fire. "Oh, and it's going to be at a Cathedral in New York with over two hundred guests!"

"Shh," Gary soothed, rocking her gently from side to side. "Nothing has changed, kitten. I promise you. If I had known what my mother was up to, I never would have allowed her to buy the dress."

Clinging to him, Candy sobbed. "I can't believe this is happening. She even hired a limo to drive us around while we were there!" The rocking stopped, and she peeked up at him. "That didn't surprise you, did it?"

"Candy, I have to tell you something," he replied softly.

"What?" she bit sharply, her nerves raw.

Stroking the hair off of her forehead, he stared down into her clear hazel eyes. When had his life become so complicated? He had walked away from his parents' dreams a long time ago, headed out on his own, and followed his own path. Why should marrying this girl change any of that?

Swallowing hard, he knew why. "I'm sure you've noticed that my family is well off," he stated calmly.

"You mean that they're rich?" she replied, extricating herself from his arms. "Yeah, I noticed." Their differences from other people were obvious and always had been.

"Rich." He chuckled, turning to the back yard and leaning against the railing as he admired the nearly bare trees. "My family is more than rich, baby."

Staring at his back, Candy frowned, causing deep lines to crinkle her forehead. "Have they disowned you?"

Hesitating, her question sounded odd in light of his mother's phone call before he left the office. "No. But my mother thinks you are only here to get your share of my family's wealth."

"What the hell!" Candy squealed, grabbing his arm and pulling him to face her. "She said that? And you think she's right, don't you!"

"I never said that." He raised his hands to wave her off. "She thinks that you didn't protest enough about the wedding. You let her drop almost twenty grand on an event she didn't even want to take place and that it's proof that your meek and meager demeanor is just a ruse. You were playing hard to get, and this is exactly what you wanted all along." His mother had had plenty more to say on the matter, but he stopped there, at least for the time being.

"I don't believe this," she whispered, her eyes wide as she stared up at him. "A surrealistic nightmare, that's where I am. Caught in a web I have no hope of escaping. I think the wedding is off, Gary."

"Don't say that!" He clasped her arms and pulled her onto her tip-toes. "Please, Candy. I've been so patient. Waited so long. Let's get married just like we planned. To hell with my mother and her stupid suspicions. I don't believe a word of it, and I'm not going to let her run my life! I never have, and I never will."

"How can I believe that, Gary? You let her take me to New York. What was I supposed to do? Scream at her in the middle of some fancy dress shop that I didn't want her ugly gown? Or that her caterer was way more than I was comfortable with? And that cake... Oh my God! I didn't want any of that. I only let her do it so I didn't cause a scene. I wanted to be respectful. So I get accused of being a what...a gold digger?"

It had never occurred to her to ask how much Gary or his family was worth, and she wasn't about to do so now. Still, if it were as much as she now suspected, she definitely needed to get out while she still could. Pulling away from him, she wiped at her tears. "I'll find an apartment for us by the end of the month," she stated flatly.

"The hell you will!" he tossed back in a fit of rage. "You don't even have a job, Candy. Your mother is in poor health, and your son is in the best place for him. The last thing you're going to do is uproot everyone over something as stupid as this!"

Crossing her arms over her chest, she squeezed herself, hoping to appear stronger than she felt. "I can get a job," she whispered, realizing immediately that if she did, it would mean the end of her schooling. *Damn.* An entire year, and she really wasn't any better off than she had been. It had all been an illusion.

Holding up his palms, Gary rocked his jaw from side to side, then begged, "Baby, let's think this through, ok? You and Lanelle and Daks. This is your home. If anyone has to leave, it's going to be me."

Candy's wet orbs shot up to glare at him. "What do you mean by that?" she demanded curtly.

"It means I'm going to sign this house over to you. And I'll set up a stipend for you to live on. I don't need my salary from the fire department, and I never did. I could live the rest of my life and never work another day. I love my job," he confessed, his voice growing lower with every word that he spoke.

"I know you do." She nodded slightly. "I don't want your house…or your money. I don't even know why we're talking about this." Her lip quivered violently as tears gushed over and streaked her flushed cheeks. She wanted to fling herself into his arms and beg his forgiveness. For what, she had no idea, but she felt as if all of this were somehow her fault.

Afraid to touch her, Gary agreed, "I don't know either, baby. But I can tell you on December twentieth, I'll be standing in that living room in front of that fireplace…if you'll have me." He wouldn't trade his chance to marry Candice Parker for all the gold in the world, and he hoped like hell they could work it out.

Her nose bright red from crying, she stared up at him. A pitiful sight, Gary's stomach lurched at the thought of where they now stood—on the edge of calling it quits. Reaching for her, he pulled her slowly towards him. Lowering his lips to hers, he kissed her lightly.

The tingle that passed between them surprised her. Candy had been afraid that she wouldn't be enough woman for him when they got down to it, with where she had come from and the fear she still carried inside her. Parting her lips, she allowed the kiss to deepen, the sweetness of his taste drawing her in further. Her hands finding his shoulders, her fingers kneaded the muscles beneath his coat, and she heard herself sigh a soft moan. She had never felt desire—not like this.

Breaking their connection but only by a few inches, she asked quietly, "Are you sure this is what you want? Maybe your mother is right. Maybe this is all one huge bad idea."

"My mother is definitely not right, and I would give up everything I own to have you as my wife," he replied without batting an eye. "If you give me the chance, I'm going to prove it to you one day at a time."

FIVE

Righting the Past

TAPE MEASURE IN HAND, Candice plotted the layout of the large living area on a notepad. They would be bringing in chairs for the ceremony, and she would need to know exactly how much room they were going to have.

"Who can that be?" she mumbled to herself when a sharp knock at the door interrupted her thoughts. Laying her tools and notes aside, she peeked out the window and then opened the door.

"Hi, Candy," a short, dark-haired man said when she stood before him.

Staring at the young man, she felt confused. Things had leveled out over the last week after Gary had put his foot down with his mother and her wild plans, or at least she thought they had. However, standing there with a stranger before her, who clearly knew who she was, threw that prospect into doubt.

"Can I help you?" her voice shook as her mind

raced. He looked familiar in an odd sort of way, but she decided firmly against saying so.

"Candy, it's me, Cliff." He smiled as he spoke, his tone growing hushed. "Dakota's father."

Blinking rapidly, Candice fought to process the phrase. *Dakota's father*. Arriving at nothing, she stammered, "What do you want, Cliff? I have class in an hour, and I need to catch the bus."

The young man glanced at his watch rapidly, then suggested, "Maybe I can give you a ride. I really need to talk to you. It's kind of urgent."

Glancing over her shoulder, her heart thumped loudly inside her chest. "Wait here," she requested, practically closing the door in his face before she snapped the lock into place. *Cliff*. The name familiar, she had no doubt that he had been right. Although she had no idea who exactly had been Daks' father at the time of his birth, she had grown confident as he grew and his features became distinctive. *Shit, what the hell is he doing here?*

Leaving her map and measuring for later, she located her book bag and peeked in on her mother, who had lain down for her afternoon nap. She would get up shortly before the school bus dropped Dakota off at the end of the driveway and sit with him until Gary arrived home and started dinner.

This was her late class, so she wouldn't be home until close to nine when Cathy dropped her off.

Closing her mother's door, she exited by the back, locking that door as well and pocketing the key, along with her phone. Walking around to the front, the hairs on the back of her neck prickled as she considered taking a ride with the near stranger. Strolling up to him, she decided she needed a few answers before she climbed into his car.

"How did you find me?" she demanded in as even a tone as she could muster.

"It wasn't easy." He grinned. "I had to get a lawyer, and he helped me file the paperwork to get a paternity test."

Candy grew stiff, unaware of any such test ever having been performed. "When was this?" she demanded more sharply. "I didn't put your name on his birth certificate."

"Nope, you left it blank." He tossed his dark curls and indicated his antique Mustang parked along the street. "If you'll hop in, I can talk fast while I get you over to the JC."

Moving slowly, the girl complied against her better judgment. She didn't feel a hundred percent safe riding around with him, but the thought of his being there when her son arrived home spurred her on. The last thing she wanted was a confrontation before she knew what he wanted.

"So, you got a paternity test," she said more calmly as she snapped her seatbelt into place. "And how did that go?"

"Like I said, I'm Dakota's father." He grinned widely. "Relax, Candy. I'm not here to hurt you or to mess anything up for you. I'm gettin' my life straight. I felt really bad after everything that happened back when he was born, an' I wanna make it up to you. Both of you."

Curling her tongue, the girl wondered if he was sincere. "Why didn't you say anything then?"

"Like what?" He chortled, pulling into a parking lot and shutting off the engine. "Like, 'yeah, me and my six buddies are all bangin' her?' That woulda been pleasant. Especially after you didn't tell anyone, including your mother."

"Stop it, Cliff." Candy's eyes cut over at him, sharp as daggers. "You have no idea what I told them!"

"Ah, Candy." He toyed with the leather cover on his steering wheel. "I know why you didn't say anything. I mean, I know you only did it because we pressured you to. It was a game, and you finally got caught. I really appreciated you not ratting me out, though."

Her lips formed a stiff line as she pressed them together. "So what are you doing here?"

"I told you. I'm getting my life straight. Righting the past, so to speak. I've had six years to get my shit together, an' I figure I owe it to our son to be there for him." He paused, shooting her a quick glance. "I mean, you and me were never really a thing, but I'm still his daddy."

Sharp emotion sliced through her gut. *Daddy*. She hadn't pushed the issue, but she had hoped one day Daks would call Gary by that name. "You may be his father, but you won't ever be his *daddy*."

Snickering, he pressed harder, "Well, I guess you

don't need to see the report then. You know I'm right, so why are you makin' a fuss?"

"I don't know anything, Cliff, except that this is not my school. I really do have class," she stated more calmly than she felt. She hadn't let anyone know where she was going, and if anything happened, no one would even know she was missing for hours. *Until I don't show up to catch my ride with Cathy after my class.*

By then, it would be too late.

Still playing with the hole in the steering wheel cover, Cliff appeared unmoved. "Relax. It's only Junior College. Missing one night ain't gonna kill you," he surmised. "I just wanna talk to you for a bit."

Shifting in her seat, Candy wondered if he was being honest with her, or even himself. What if he thought there *had been* something between them? "What is it that you want? Tell me exactly."

"I want to see my son." He nodded firmly as he spoke. "I want you to introduce me to him. And I wanna set up visitation."

The very word visitation almost stopped her heart with fear. "You're a stranger to him. He won't want to go with you."

She could see the muscle in the side of his jaw flex, and she tried to explain. "Daks was hurt when he was born. We were both sick, and he won't ever be normal. He's about two years old, mentally speaking. His understanding of the world will never be like ours. He isn't going to understand."

Cliff twisted in the seat and glared at her, his eyes wide and lips pursed into a twisted pout.

He didn't say a word, and he didn't have to; cold terror froze her into the seat. She couldn't move to get her phone, and she prayed she wouldn't need it.

"It's nothing against you!" she smoothed quickly. "It's him. That's just the way he is. I'm not making it up. I swear to you!"

"Get out," her cohort stated gruffly.

"What do you mean, get out? You said you would take me to the school!"

"An' you said you would take the bus, so get on it, whore."

Dumbfounded, Candy stared at him. "What gives you the right to speak to me that way?"

"Get out. And this conversation never took place, you get me?" he snarled, cranking the key.

Reaching for the handle, Candy didn't argue.

Fear gripped her gut as she stumbled out and slammed the door. Looking around, she wasn't entirely sure where she even was, but she knew one thing; anywhere would be safer than sitting in that car with Dakota's father.

SIX

Macho Man

AFTER WATCHING Cliff spin the tires of his bright red Mustang as he drove away, Candy chose a path and began walking. Finding a street sign at the corner, she realized where he had dumped her and felt calmer, about that at least. As for the rest, she needed some serious alone time.

Walking a few blocks from the parking lot, she entered a small sports bar and ordered a sensible dinner. She knew she should find a way to class, but her gut told her it would be a lost cause. *What I really need is some time to think.*

Remaining at the pub and nursing her drink after she had eaten, her mind raced. From Gary's mother to Cliff showing up, nothing had gone as they had planned since they made their announcement at Halloween, and she was afraid it would give her an ulcer if she wasn't careful.

Eventually, she knew she needed to get home and called herself a cab. Of course, showing up at the house in the unusual ride only left her with a great deal of explaining to do, and Gary met her at the door.

As soon as she entered, he confronted her, his eyes wide with angry fear and demanding, "What the hell happened to Cathy giving you a ride? She called a few minutes ago looking for you. And why didn't you answer your phone for either of us?"

Swallowing hard, Candy braced herself for the flood of additional questions she knew would follow her reply. "Dakota's father showed up today," she confessed as evenly as she could muster.

His forehead crinkled, Gary looked as if he'd been punched. "His father? After all this time? What did he want? What did he say? Have you been with him this whole time?"

The confusion on his features was enough to crush her, and Candy spilled her guts about the entire afternoon and evening. Starting with opening the door and finding him on their porch, she left out no detail until she stepped out of the cab a few minutes ago. "As far as the phone, I didn't hear it ring. I swear. I would never have let you or Cathy worry on purpose," she whined.

"Are you out of your mind? I don't believe you left with him. And he didn't tell you anything else?"

"No. That was it."

"And you sat at a bar all night, just thinking about it," his voice grew louder, nearing a shout.

"Gary, please!" Candy begged as he stomped around their living room. "Dakota is asleep. We don't want to wake him!"

"Don't want to wake him," her fiancé fumed. "I can't believe you didn't get more out of that guy! I'll hire a PI and see if we can find out more about him."

"We don't need to do that." She folded her hands together, interlocking her fingers as if to pray. "He said the conversation never took place. I shouldn't ever have told you about it!" she lamented, having never seen him this upset.

Gary spun on his heel to face her. Towering more than a foot above her, he struggled to maintain his cool exterior. "Don't you know a threat when you hear one? He clearly has no respect for you, and if I had been there, he damn sure would have gotten his attitude adjusted!"

Her posture sagging, she turned her back on him. Pressing her right palm to her forehead, she felt feverish. "I'm not scared for me. I'm scared for Daks. He isn't going to understand. I tried to explain that to him, but he didn't care."

"Of course he didn't care. He was having sex with an underage girl and got her pregnant. That's the reason he didn't speak up when Dakota was born. He would have gone to jail if he had. The only question is, why is he here now? I can't see how any good will come from this." Gary's voice shifted from anger to sorrow. On the outside, he looked like any other macho man, but deep down, he cared deeply for Candy and her son. "God, baby, if anything had happened to you today!"

"Nothing happened to me today." She sighed, turning to face him. "Except that I missed class. I don't know why he's here. I can only assume that he really wants to spend time with his son. I can also only assume that he has no idea what he's getting into."

"Because Dakota is no ordinary kid," Gary surmised.

"Exactly. You got to know him first. And you had a choice. Cliff is stuck with him. He may not be able to handle the fact that Daks won't ever be like other sons. There won't be any ball games or little league. No soccer or any of that. Daks is never going to grow up, and he won't ever be like other kids."

"I see." He nodded, stepping over and drawing her against him. Laying his cheek against the top of her head, he breathed loudly. "Please don't ever get into a car with a strange man again. I don't care who he is."

"I promise," she replied with a sniff, aware of what her choice could have cost them. "Do you really think we need to find out more about him?"

"Absolutely." He straightened to look her in the eye. "I don't think my mother would have anything to do with this. The connection just doesn't reach. But with everything else that has been going on and the wedding coming up, we can't be too careful."

Nodding her approval, Candy agreed in a hoarse whisper, "I'll tell them what I know. And maybe Mom can remember a few things that might help. I hate to get her involved in this with her health the way that it is."

"We don't really have a choice, baby." He pulled

her in close once more. "But to be on the safe side, let's not tell anyone else about it, at least not until we know exactly what we're dealing with. You'll have to make up some excuse for Cathy, but you'll think of something."

"Agreed," she lamented. She had not relished the idea of explaining Dakota's existence to Gary's family in the first place. Knowing that his father could be a crazed lunatic did not make the prospect any more appealing.

SEVEN

Silver Foxes

"I UNDERSTAND. YES." Gary spoke into the phone as Candy quietly listened.

Holding a letter that had been hand-delivered to her that morning, her hand shook as she read the words again: ORDER TO APPEAR.

"Ok, Monday then, at nine a.m. Thank you, sir," Gary said before he hung up the phone and faced her. "That's it. We have an attorney."

Tearing her eyes from the page, she stared up at him dolefully. "He's going to take my son."

"He isn't going to take anything," he soothed as he gently relieved her of the summons. "There is no way a judge or jury or anyone for that matter would choose to give Dakota to Cliff Barnes. End of story."

"You don't know that," she stammered. "What if they don't like how I handled things? What if they think I should have told him about Daks from the beginning?"

"Don't worry about the things you can't change, kitten." He stroked her cheek. "My parents will be here in an hour for our Thanksgiving dinner. Go wash your face and put on something pretty."

"You want me to dress up for them?" she hissed in shock.

"No." He chuckled. "I want you to dress up for you. It'll make you feel better."

"What about Daks? Mom will be back inside with him any minute, and he will probably need changed after being outside," she insisted.

"As cool as it is, I'm sure he didn't get too dirty. Maybe played on the swings a bit is all. But if he needs changed, I'll handle it. Now go." He turned her and swatted her behind for good measure.

Smiling in spite of herself, Candy trudged up the stairs. Enjoying a hot shower, she leaned against the wall, allowing the water to trickle over her until her skin had begun to wrinkle. Stepping out, she glanced at the scale and recalled that she hadn't weighed in a few weeks. Her diet and exercise had all but fallen by the wayside since Halloween and their big announcement.

Stepping onto the device, she gasped at the number glaring back at her. She had been afraid she might have gained some of her weight back, but on the contrary, she had lost even more. Perhaps she hadn't been eating enough after all. Celebrating by slipping into a new lacy pair of panties and matching bra, she smiled at herself in the full-length mirror that stood in the corner of her bedroom.

She really hadn't intended to lose weight when she first changed her diet and began her morning runs. On the contrary, she had been content with her plump self and her pudgy fingers. She had only wanted to feel better and more in control of her body and life.

But when the first few pounds had melted away, it had changed something inside her. It felt like a drug, the euphoric feeling that came with a new, lower number, and she quickly latched onto ways to get more of it.

Using both hands, she placed them around her waist and grinned at how close the tips of her fingers lay. *It was a good change, no matter the reason.* She had no intention of gaining the weight back, that was for sure, and hoped that Gary would be pleased with her lighter form when the time came for him to see the goods.

Turning to her closet, she located a pretty print dress that she had found on a clearance rack a few weeks before. Although it wasn't really a holiday style, she didn't care at the moment. It did make her feel better to enjoy the silky material against her soft skin, and she smiled that Gary had suggested it. She loved that man so much. He had become her rock, and she hoped he would be so for many years to come.

Descending the stairs a short time later, she discovered Dakota on the floor of the den, playing with his firetruck, the one that Gary had given him last year for Christmas. Leaning on the doorframe with a small grin curling her lips, she watched him swing it around and spray the couch with imaginary water.

"Such a happy young man." Roger startled her when he spoke over her shoulder.

Looking up at the senior Ford, Candy smiled at the clear blue eyes of Gary's father. His hair a shiny grey, she thought about how she had often thought of him as a silver fox, with his rugged good looks and well-kept physique. The two of them had never spoken for any length of time, and it felt odd to her that he would do so now.

"I think he's happy," she agreed noncommittally. "I better see if Gary needs help with dinner."

"Let Eve help with dinner. She needs to get her hands dirty every once in a while." Roger grinned deviously. "I'd like to have a talk with you if you don't mind." He waved a hand towards the front of the house, and she turned and led the way to the living room.

Spying the generous fire, Candice moved to stand in front of it, aware of the steel blue eyes that watched her as she did so. Warming her fingers, she rubbed her hands together a few times, but he said nothing. "You don't much approve of me," she finally stated flatly before she turned around.

"I never said that." Roger lifted his chin. "Candy, allow me to be blunt," he said in a quiet tone as he sidled closer to her. "Gerald has informed me of this rough business with Dakota's father. There is no way such a man can ever be allowed to take a child from his mother. He assures me that our family attorney has accepted the case, and I have every confidence that this issue will be resolved. Timely and justly."

Running her tongue around her teeth for a moment, she stalled, then replied, "Thank you. I was under the impression that we weren't going to burden others with our troubles, especially with tomorrow being a holiday."

"It's no burden, Candy," his deep voice cajoled her. "You are practically family."

She chuckled at his words. "Forgive me, but I doubt that your wife will ever see it that way."

"Yes, well"—the older man flashed his perfect white teeth—"Eve is a stubborn woman. She and Gary never have seen eye to eye. I'm sure being told she would never have any other children played heavily in that. Something about knowing all your hopes and dreams rest on a single pair of shoulders, to be precise."

She smiled more fully, a feeling of confidence overtaking her. "We've never really talked before. I guess I assumed you also had someone else picked out for your son and that I didn't measure up."

"That's not for me to decide." His hand found her arm and gave her a squeeze. "Take care of my son. And yours. That's all that I ask. If you do those things, you will be more than good enough."

Releasing her, he turned and strolled to the kitchen to let himself out the back for a smoke on his pipe. Watching him go, Candy considered how kind and caring he appeared to be and wondered if that had been where Gary got his strong, devoted personality, as it obviously hadn't come from Eve.

EIGHT

A Mother's Dreams

EVE TOYED with the linen tablecloth while waiting for Gary to join her. She knew that something was going on—something he had shared with her husband but had chosen not to reveal to her. Whatever it was, she intended to find out.

Smiling up at him when he approached and claimed his seat, she said in a low hiss, "Darling, you work too hard at that job of yours."

"I like my job, Mother," he replied coolly. "And I'm sure that's not why you invited me to lunch."

Waving at the waiter, she ignored the presumed jab. "How are the wedding plans coming along? Is everything set for the big day?" she asked after their orders had been placed.

"That is going very well." He grinned despite his discomfort. "We've arranged for a judge to do the honors, and it will take place in the front room as originally planned. Candy has chosen what she calls a 'sensible' dress, but she hasn't allowed me to see it."

"Of course not." His mother laughed aloud. "It would be bad luck if you did."

Tapping the tips of his fingers against one another, he waited. When she said nothing more, he confessed, "I thought surely you had something up your sleeve when you invited me here. Care to tell me what it is, or should I continue guessing?"

"Oh, Gary," she chortled. "You always were direct, if anything. I wanted to talk about your future. I was serious about your job. You've stalled long enough. I really want you to accept the VP position when Omar retires. It's time that you learned the ropes since you well know you will be running the place soon enough."

Leaning back in his chair, Gary ran his fingers anxiously around his lips. They had had this conversation at least once a year for the better part of a decade, and he still wondered if she had coerced his great aunt into leaving him the house as some sort of master plan to get her way. Finally, pointing a stiff index finger at her, he stated, "You never give up, do you?"

"A mother's dreams are all that she has." Eveline swirled her glass of wine. "Do you think it was easy…letting you go?"

"What's that supposed to mean?"

"When you left home, that army thing and then the policeman thing and then the fire thing…" Her voice trailed away, a distant look in her eye. "Did it never occur to you how much I worried over you? No calls. No letters. No nothing. An occasional holiday if

I pressed the issue. And then you up and want to marry some girl who is clearly beneath us."

"That's enough!" Gary sat straight up. "You can call me anything you want, but you won't talk that way about Candy. She's a good woman. A good mother to her son. You don't know her like I do, and you have no…"

The waiter arrived at the table, effectively ending his tirade. Moving his arms to allow his plate to be placed before him, he glared at the woman across from him.

When they were alone again, he continued in a quieter tone, "She isn't beneath us. We aren't better than other people because we have money. Luckier, maybe. But not better." Gary had struggled with that issue most of his life and had found peace in giving back to those around him—something his mother never had understood.

"What happened to her that makes you so protective?" Eveline asked in a curious tone. "You never did like girls who could take care of themselves. Not for long, anyway."

"You've got to be kidding me." Gary chuckled and picked up his fork. "Candy is damn sure capable of taking care of herself. When I met her, she was working in a convenience store to make ends meet for the three of them."

"And you still don't think she sees you as the easy way out?" his mother sneered.

"No, I don't. For starters, I was just a fireman in her eyes, and she hated it. I practically begged her to date me, but she refused. I only worked my way in with her after the fire that put them on the street, and that took a hell of a lot out of her to allow me to help," he stated more calmly.

"All right. Let's assume for a moment that you're right. Her actions have been purely innocent. What's going on then? I know you met with our attorney Monday, but your father won't tell me a thing. Is it a prenup?" Her eyes glistened with the prospect of gleaning a shred of useful information from him.

Sighing loudly, Gary rolled his eyes and used his glass of wine to wash down his last bite of lasagna, a practice he knew that his mother detested. Watching her mouth twist as she fought to hold her rebuke, he grinned. "You always were easy to get rolling."

"And you were an insolent little ass." She pushed her chair back, ready to walk away.

"Just…relax." He waved a palm at her. "I'll tell you what you want to know, but it needs to stay between us for the time being." Taking another drink of his beverage, he sighed. "Candy's in trouble. Daks' father showed up and is threatening to take him away from her."

Her eyes wide, Eve gripped the arms of her chair firmly. Nothing he could have said would have struck her more deeply than a mother's pain. "When did this happen?" she demanded in a quiet tone. "And why didn't you tell me?"

"We decided to keep it quiet, that's all." He shrugged. "I only talked to Dad because I wanted his advice. It happened after your little trip to New York, so Candy is more than a little freaked out about it."

"And?" She adjusted her grip as if the seat might toss her onto the floor at any moment.

"And she was just a kid when they were together. Her father had died in the line of duty, and her mother was all that she had left. The bastard took advantage of her, a fifteen-year-old girl, and then left her hanging out to dry when Dakota was born," Gary simplified, not feeling as if she needed the grimy details. "Anyway, he's filed for custody. We have a hearing the week after Christmas, which has put a real damper on things—both the coming holiday and the wedding."

Eve watched her son silently for several minutes. He picked at his food, occasionally eating a bite, but she could see he had been deeply troubled by what he had shared. "You really love that girl, don't you?" she finally stated in a quiet tone.

"Nice." He coughed a small laugh. "I've only been saying that I do for about a year. Glad I finally convinced you." Dropping his napkin on his plate, he stood to leave.

"Gary, wait." His mother looked up at him with large pleading brown orbs. "Is there anything I can do to help?"

"Like what, Mom?" He shoved his hands in his pockets and rocked onto his heels.

"I don't know." She appeared flustered. "Is there anything that she needs? A character witness? Some dirt on this guy?"

Managing a grin, Gary shook his head. "I think we'll be ok. We're focusing on the wedding, and we'll deal with Daks' father when the time comes. Until then, we'll let our attorney handle all that." He bent over and kissed her softly on the cheek. "I'll see you at the wedding," he tossed over his shoulder as he headed for the exit.

NINE

What It Takes

TURNING TO WATCH HIM GO, Eve's mind raced. She had hated Candy since the first time they met. She wanted to say it was because the girl did not deserve her son, or he deserved better, or something of that nature.

However, it had largely been because she realized it had been the girl's fault he had not kept his appointment for Christmas dinner last year. She was Gary's mother after all. She had a right to be angry, didn't she? She only saw her son once or twice a year, and missing out on one of those occasions was certainly enough reason to be upset.

Chewing the side of her finger for a moment, she caught sight of the waiter and motioned for their check. She needed to get moving, with a new list of stops to make replacing her afternoon of shopping, and the first one would be the hardest.

She felt certain their attorney wasn't going to share what he knew willingly. She would need a plan, and maybe even a little blackmail, if she was going to find out who this man was that had threatened her son's happiness as if he could get away with it.

Arriving at the brick-clad office a short time later, Eveline put her nose in the air and sauntered inside. Stopping in front of the secretary's desk, she announced smugly, "Good afternoon, Caroline. I need to see Benjamin, and no, I don't have an appointment. It's an emergency."

Her jaw dropped at the older woman's audacity, the petite blonde pointed at a chair. "Have a seat, Mrs. Ford, and I'll let Ben know that you're here."

Turning with a flourish, Eve perched on the edge of the seat. Keeping her chin up, she did her best to present an air of confidence—one she did not feel. After her confrontation with Gary, she knew the danger of losing her son was real and not because of Candy—well not exactly because of her, at any rate.

Gary was completely devoted to the girl, and it tore him apart to see her unhappy that Daks' father wanted to take him away. Even worse, Eveline knew that her son made an excellent father to the boy, looking after him while his mother attended class and the like. Where had this stranger been all this time, and why suddenly show up making demands?

She had smelled a rat when Gary had first announced their intentions to wed, but perhaps she had been picking up the wrong trail. It could be that this fellow claiming to be Daks' father somehow knew of their plans and intended to use their relationship to get to her family's wealth. It seemed feasible, and that would be her next stop as soon as she had his address—to find out if he could be bought. And if so, what the price would be.

"Eveline," Ben's voice interrupted her thoughts. "How lovely to see you. My third Ford in less than a week. Please, come in." He offered her the entrance to his office.

"Third, am I? This must be more serious than I feared," she admitted quietly as he closed the door behind them. "Please, what can you tell me?" she got straight to the point.

"I can't really tell you anything, Eve. You know that," he countered evenly. "This is a private matter between Candy and Gary, and the court. As I explained to Roger yesterday, my hands are tied until the hearing."

"Ben, be sensible. You know that I always handle the dirty work in this family. I'll do whatever it takes to settle this. All I need is a name and address, and you don't have to worry about anything else." She grinned slyly as she spoke.

Hesitating, her adversary stared at her over the top of his glasses, waiting to see if she would change her statement. Finally, he asked, "Should I ask for a retainer…in case you do anything stupid?"

"No." She cackled. "It's not like I'm going to kill him. I just need to speak to him…in private."

"I don't think that's a good idea," Ben shook his head as he spoke. "I know you're an ace at the bargaining table, but this isn't your fight. And it really isn't Gary's. In the end, Candy is the one this man is after, and why is hard to say. He has filed a petition for sole custody on the grounds that she's an unfit mother. That's a hard claim to prove, and I have every confidence we will win. He'll be lucky if he can even get visitation, but we have to let justice run its course. I'm sorry, Eve. I really wish I could help, but my hands are tied."

"Ben, I hear what you're saying, but we can't wait. Gary and Candy are getting married on the twentieth, and this needs to be settled before then." She looked up at him with large, pleading brown eyes.

"You think this is a ploy and your bank account is his real target," Ben stated, his finger waggling in the air. "We don't have any proof of that."

"I don't need any proof," she insisted. "All I need is to talk to him. Or better yet, draft an agreement for me. One that I can present to this guy and see if he can be bought."

Ben's eyebrows shot up. "You want to offer Cliff a bribe?"

Eve smiled at the drop of the name, her first concrete clue in her inquiry. "Not in so many words. I want to see if there is an arrangement that we can reach—one that he would be happy to stand behind and allow Gary and Candy to keep her son."

Shaking his head, Benjamin muttered, "You're some piece of work, Eveline Ford. Hard to believe you actually married into the family with balls like those." Moving to his computer, he pulled up a document and adjusted a few lines. "This should do the trick. If he signs it, Candy will need to agree to it as well. Then, bring it back to me, and I'll contact his attorney from here."

"Arbitration," she read at the top of the form.

"Yes, it means that both parties met with a mediator and came to an agreement. It's perfectly legal and binding, so if he agrees, he can't change his mind later."

"Good." Eve chuckled. "So where do I find him?" Accepting the sticky note with the address penned across it, she grinned. "Thanks, Ben. I knew you wouldn't let me down."

TEN

Deal of a Lifetime

GIVING HER DRIVER THE ADDRESS, Eve leaned
into the back seat and watched the houses passing by
as they entered a residential area. Glad she had
brought the BMW rather than the limo, she considered that even it stuck out like a sore thumb in the
run-down community.

Arriving in front of a white house with asbestos
shingles, she observed that it had seen better days.
The small chain-link fence in front of it sagged in
places, and the piece next to the missing gate had
been torn down completely. Glaring at the antique red
Mustang parked in the drive, she shook her head in
disgust. Swallowing, she considered that even
knocking on such a dwelling could be dangerous.

Gathering her courage, Eve opened her door and
stepped out, her flowing dress and fur coat held
firmly by her trembling hands as she marched up to
the steps. Knocking soundly on the wooden door
frame, she waited. The wooden door opened, and a

short, dark-haired man stood staring at her through the haze of the rusted screen.

"Can I help you?" Cliff asked in a surly tone, scratching at his chest through his white undershirt as he spoke.

"I'm Eveline Ford," she informed him succinctly. "I'm looking for Cliff Barnes."

"That's me," he muttered, pushing against the screen and holding it open for her to enter. "You might not wanna sit down." He chuckled. "Might mess up those fancy clothes o' yours."

Glancing around at the meager accommodations, Eve briefly considered walking away. There was no way he could win his case living in such squalor, but an instant later, she knew she couldn't risk it. Daks' future, and thereby Candy's, must be secured at all costs.

"Mr. Barnes, I'll get straight to the point. I'm here to offer a settlement—to negotiate a deal between you and Candy over the custody of Dakota."

"Uh-huh," he grunted, still scratching at the dirty shirt.

"Yes. I'm sure you are aware that if Candy retains custody, that you will be required to pay support for the boy, and she will be required to allow you visitation," Eve spoke in a matter-of-fact tone.

"Yeah, but she ain't gonna win. She's been shacked up with that guy for a year, and my lawyer says that fathers have rights these days." He grinned.

"Mr. Barnes, Candy is a good mother, and Gary has been a good father figure to Dakota. Removing him from their home would only serve to harm the boy. Nonetheless, that is why I am here. To discern what it would take for you to withdraw your request," she clipped.

Rocking his jaw in a slow circle, Cliff considered her words before he replied, "Are you here to offer me money? I may sound like a dumb hick, but that don't mean that I am," he sneered. "You in your fancy clothes and car, and that big ass house they're livin' in. I got rights, too."

Not rattled by his angry words, Eve lowered her voice to make her offer. "Yes, you have rights. You obviously care very deeply about Dakota and have his best interests at heart. I'm prepared to offer you a stipend. Twenty-five thousand a year. It will cover your child support and leave you with a small amount to better your living conditions for when you have visitation."

Cliff grinned broadly. "A stipend! Is that like a payment for free, or whatta I gotta do to get it?"

"Yes, it's a payment to you." Eveline lifted her chin slightly. "All you have to do is drop your custody suit. Everyone signs, agreeing to the amount and conditions, and the case is closed. You get paid, you get visitation, and Candy keeps her son."

Turning in a slow circle, Cliff's features morphed into a gloat while his back was to her. He hadn't anticipated winning so easily, and greed crept into his heart. Screwing his lips into a more acceptable smile, he faced her squarely. "I'll take two hundred an' fifty K."

Her breath caught in her lungs, Eve faltered, "What's that supposed to mean?"

"It means I want you to pay me that much. Two hundred and fifty thousand. Give me that, and I'll go away."

"That's quite a jump—ten times what you were offered," she stated angrily. *How dare he be so brazen? So callous about his son's future!*

"It's the same thing, just in a lump sum. And I'll leave him alone and let Candy and that son o' yours have him, even adopt him if he wants to. You can sever my rights, an' it'll be like I never existed." Cliff's eyes glistened. He never dreamed it would be this easy.

"Very well." Eveline sighed. "You drive a hard bargain, Mr. Barnes," she lied flatly, keenly aware he had sold out much cheaper than she would have paid to settle the matter. "I have a page here." She presented her form. "Do you have a table where we can fill in the details of our agreement?"

"Right this way, Madam." He wafted a hand as he ushered her into his kitchen. Clearing a spot on the table by swiping food crumbs onto the floor, he beamed. "You won't regret this."

"I'm sure I won't," she agreed, eyeing the sink full of dirty dishes and spatter-coated stove. Bending over the page and not daring to sit, she quickly penned the outline of their agreement and presented it to him. "Read it and be sure I've included everything," she commanded.

Looking over the details, he grinned broadly.

"That's a sweet deal…for both of us. Candy's sure lucky, though. Gettin' to marry that rich guy. Quite a jump from the whore she was in her younger days."

Her lips pursed, Eve held her tongue. Allowing him to sign the page, she snarled, "Thank you, Mr. Barnes. Candy's attorney will be in contact with yours, and we will have this filed right away."

"Yeah, you do that," he shot back. "When do I get paid?"

"Soon." She nodded, folding the page and tucking it inside a pocket in her coat next to her chest. "Very soon." At that moment, she wondered if it would have been more prudent to have hired a hit on him instead, despite Benjamin's concern.

ELEVEN

Share the Wealth

GETTING up from her computer and stretching exaggeratedly, Candy made her way downstairs for a cup of coffee. Her last final coming the next day, she wanted an A and had been going over the entire semester worth of notes. *Damn. I never knew how hard school could be as an adult.* As a kid, it had seemed so easy.

Arriving at the bottom of the stairs, she discovered Daks and Gary rolling around on the floor. Getting on all fours, Gary scrunched down, and Daks scrambled onto his back. Then Gary crawled around as Daks clung to his shirt for dear life while squealing, "Horsey, horsey," until he fell off and they had to start over.

"How long have you two been at this?" she finally asked after their third trip around the room.

"A while." Gary laughed, rolling the boy over and goosing his belly to peals of laughter. "Wanna get some ice cream?"

"I gave up ice cream, remember?" she muttered a bit tartly.

"I wasn't talking to you." He poked the boy again and demanded, "You want some ice cream, huh, huh?"

"Imeans! Imeans!" Dakota laughed while struggling to get to his feet.

"All right. Let's load up and get to the store before the snow starts."

Candy wanted to jump in and go with them, but for an instant, she felt sad that she hadn't been invited. Remembering her studies with a sigh, she knew it was for the best anyways. *Besides, if we lose custody of him, this will be a special memory for Gary.* A tear formed in her eye as the thought sank in about the uncertainty of their future. "You guys be careful," she called over her shoulder as she headed into the kitchen to hide her sadness.

Pouring her cup, she could see the light on in her mother's room. Peeking in, Lanelle sat propped up in her bed, presumably reading the book on her lap. "Hey, Mom," she said softly, half hoping the woman wouldn't reply and she could slip back upstairs.

"Hey, baby." Lanelle looked up and smiled at her. "Come and sit with me," she invited warmly as she patted the empty side of the bed.

Making her way through the small sitting area, Candy obliged, sipping her warm brew before she sat down on the pliable surface. "Whatcha reading?" she asked noncommittally.

"Oh, just a little Christmas story. Nothing

special." Her mother closed the book and laid it on the nightstand. "Sounded like good times in there."

"Yeah." Candy grinned, then took another sip. "Gary is the best father. He really is." Her lip quivered, giving her sorrow away.

"Oh, baby." Her mother reached for her, taking her hand and giving it a squeeze. "Don't you worry about that Cliff boy. He isn't going to take Daks away from you. You're a good mother, and you're right. Gary is going to be a great father to him."

"I know that's true." Candy drew a ragged breath. "But how do we prove that? I don't understand why this is happening."

"Well, Cliff is Dakota's father. He said he wants to make things right, didn't he?"

"Yeah, but stealing my son away isn't making things right." She sniffed.

"But he wants his share, doesn't he?" the older woman said soothingly.

"Yes. He wants to have him around, too. But he doesn't know Daks," Candy interjected quickly. "Once he sees how he is, he won't like it."

"You don't know that, baby. What if it doesn't bother him that Daks is special. It doesn't bother Gary. He loves the boy for who he is. Maybe his father will be the same way. In that case, you have to share," Lanelle explained.

"But it's so hard!" Actual tears spilled over, and Candice wiped at them angrily. "I liked it better the way it was!"

Laughing quietly, Lanelle shook her head slowly.

"You should know by now that things don't always stay the same, and we certainly don't get to choose the outcome every time. Make peace with Cliff, baby. Don't be afraid for Dakota. The more people he has that care about him, the richer his life will be."

Blinking rapidly, Candy stared at her mother. "I hadn't thought about that. I mean, I'm glad that Gary wants to be a part of his life. Do you really think Cliff wants to be his daddy now? I'm so scared, Mom!"

"He says he does." She gave her daughter a squeeze. "Take him on that word. You go to court in a few weeks. If you're open to sharing, things may turn out a lot better than you're thinking they will."

"That's true." A half-smile broke through. "I could share him. A little time here and there. Daks could have two daddies, I guess. I mean, lots of kids do, right? I just don't want it to be a competition between them," she muttered while drying her damp cheek.

"I don't think it will be. Dakota isn't really able to make those kinds of distinctions. Not like most of us. He only knows the goodness in people and is drawn to it. Give his father a chance, baby," the older woman suggested firmly.

Staring into her mother's pale blue orbs, she understood. "Thanks, Mom."

"Don't mention it, sweetie!" Lanelle leaned forward and gave her daughter a hug. "I've done my sharing over my lifetime. It's not a bad thing."

"I know." Candy grinned. "I feel like I've been

ignoring you now that Gary and I are involved. For years, you were my everything."

"But that's how things are meant to be." Lanelle chuckled. "Kids grow up. They fall in love and have families of their own. They aren't meant to be with their parents forever–" She stopped short, realizing what she had said.

Grabbing her mother around the neck, Candy gave her a squeeze. "It's ok, Mom. I know what you mean. Daks is special. Will always be special. Gary and I are going to be there for both of you. We promise."

Patting her arm as she held the embrace, Lanelle smiled. "You're special, too, Candy. My special girl. I'm happy for you, baby. Happy for all of us."

It was true. Candy was rich beyond her wildest dreams when it came to love and joy. *And as far as Cliff is concerned, maybe Mom's right. Maybe it is time that I shared the wealth,* she surmised as she got to her feet to get back to her studies. "Thanks, Mom," she said with a small smile on her way out of the room.

TWELVE

White Wedding

CANDY STARED at the dress hanging on the back of her door. A creamy winter white made entirely of lace, it hung just below her knees when she had tried it on, and she knew that it was the one. Her veil a simple mesh that covered her face and topped her head with cream-colored roses, she couldn't wait to wear them.

As a girl, she had stopped dreaming of such things about the time her father died. She felt as if she had lived in a dark tunnel since that night, always running, trying to escape, but there had been no light at the end. Not until Gary came into her life, and even then, she couldn't see his light for so long—hadn't wanted to see it.

Her fingers lightly caressing the lace skirt, she smiled. "We're going to have a beautiful life," she breathed. "Dreams really do come true." Dropping the fabric, she packed her backpack and headed downstairs. She wanted to get to the school early and be ready for her last exam of the year.

"Hey, Mom. Will you be ready for the holiday?" she asked cheerily, not willing to mention the wedding in fear it might spoil the magic of her mood if she did.

"Of course, dear." Her mother grinned while unfolding her cleaning rag and laying it across the edge of the sink. "Are you off this morning?"

"Yeah." Candy plucked an apple from the bowl in the center of the table. "I'll be home early, for sure, and then I'm off until January. I was thinking we should put up Gary's little tree tonight for Dakota."

"Good girl," Lanelle praised. "Don't worry. I'll be here when Daks gets home if you don't make it back in time, and I think putting up the tree would be fun." Thinking fondly of their conversation the night before, she smiled. "Have a wonderful day, sweetheart."

"Thanks. I will, Mom." Candy pulled on her coat and slung her pack over her shoulder. Exiting via the kitchen, she marched around the house and down the drive. The bus stop a few streets over, she hummed to herself as she strutted along. Above her, clouds had gathered, and there had been talk of snow for days.

"I doubt it," she mused. "They always talk about it, and then we hardly get any." Still, the idea of having a white wedding, literally, tickled her in an amusing sort of way. "Daks would enjoy it. That's for sure." Her little man loved snow, and now that she had settled how she felt about Cliff's return, it didn't seem that anything could interfere with their happiness or their plans for the future.

A few hours later, she had completed her test and lugged her bag back to the bus for the last time, at least for a few weeks. Feeling like she did well on the exam, her mood remained light as she sat next to the window and watched the flakes that had started while she was inside drifting to the ground. The earth had begun collecting the thick cover, and she knew a snowman could be in order that evening, as well as decorating the tree.

However, by the time she arrived back at her stop, the few flakes had become a white wall of ice and sleet. The wind howled as it gusted against her, and Candy struggled to keep her footing as she picked her way along the same walk that had been perfectly clear only a short time before.

"Well, this blows," she muttered to herself, then laughed at her twisted humor and unintended pun. Finally arriving at the end of the driveway, she could see her son and mother watching through the front glass, with the curtain pulled aside and the porch light on to fight against the swirling storm.

Making it to the covered veranda, she stomped her feet noisily as she clomped around to the back and entered through the kitchen. Greeted by the squeals of her son, she dropped her coat to the floor and pulled him into a warm embrace. "Glad to see my little man is home. I guess they ran the buses early?"

"Yes. They turned out an hour before schedule," Lanelle replied.

When Candy looked up, she could see the concern etched in her mother's face. "What's wrong?" she demanded, fear creeping into her voice.

"They're calling for a blizzard," her mother replied. "All of fire and rescue have been activated." She hesitated, her voice quavering. "Gary called when they deployed the offices downtown. He said you didn't answer your phone."

"Gary," Candy breathed. She had always feared that he would die in a fire, but at the moment, freezing ice appeared it could be just as deadly. "When?" She sniffed, upset she hadn't restored her ringer and had missed Gary's call.

"About thirty minutes ago. Many people are stranded, and they are working against the storm to save as many as they can," the older woman explained as she knelt next to her daughter and grandson. "Pray with me, Candy. Pray for Gary and the others."

Closing her eyes, she was already on it, and silence surrounded the trio for several minutes until Daks began to fidget. Getting to her feet, Candy began to give orders. "Run water into your tub, and I'll do the same upstairs. I need to get the emergency kit out of the basement as well. It's got the candles and stuff in it. Is the fire going?"

"Yes." Lanelle moved to obey, using a chair from the table to get to her feet. "I'll run the water. You get the kit."

Flinging open the door next to the stove, Candy switched on the light and dashed down the stairs.

Finding the large box, she hoisted it with both hands and hauled it up to the kitchen. Opening it, she located the hammer and thumbtacks for the windows. *I need the blankets,* she planned as she went.

Taking the flight up in twos, she counted the steps as she defeated them and sighed in relief when she opened the linen closet. Inside, a stack of thin blankets sat ready for just such an occasion. Tucking a few from the pile under her arm, she started with her bedroom and then moved to Dakota's, covering each window with the added layer of insulation.

When she reached Gary's room, she paused, feeling odd when she entered. In a few days, it would be their room, and panic stabbed her in the gut. "Gary," she sobbed, swiping away a few unexpected tears. "Be safe, baby," she pleaded as she hung the blanket in place and tacked it down firmly.

Taking the guest room last, she pulled the rest of the blankets from the closet and headed downstairs to treat the rest of the house. Spying her mother in the kitchen, she asked quietly, "Would you mind starting a pot of coffee? I'm sure Gary will want a cup when he gets home."

Lanelle could see the sadness in her daughter's eyes and agreed with a small nod. "He's going to be fine, baby. He'll be home before you know it."

Returning to her work, Candy silently hoped that her mother was right and that their dreams for the future would be safe after all.

THIRTEEN

Saving Grace

DAKOTA SNUGGLED in bed with his grandmother that night, and Candy took up residence on one of the couches next to the fire. The house lost power shortly after midnight, and Candy awoke to an eerie darkness only broken by the glow of a few embers in the fireplace a few hours later.

Quietly, she slipped up the stairs to unlatch the covers that unfolded to seal off the staircase. That way, at least the downstairs would stay warm. Stoking the fire and tossing on a few logs, she glanced at the stack of wood she had piled in the holder before she had lain down. Briefly considering how life in the house might have been when it had been built almost two hundred years before, she felt relieved that most days were not this hard.

Moving to the window, she peeled back a small edge and stared out into the darkness. Nothing moved but the wind, and she could still hear it howling against the house. A sadness hung over her, and she realized that there was a strong possibility that her wedding, planned to take place in three days, might not happen.

An instant later, guilt washed over her as she realized that far more important things were taking place and that one silly little missed ceremony would be low on the list when it came to disasters.

Closing the blanket back into place, she reclaimed her cushion and curled into a ball with her covers wrapped snuggly around her. Her tears refused denial, and she cried herself to sleep, thinking about the man who shared her life and hoping that he was still alive and out there, saving people in that heroic way of his.

"Candy," a deep voice called to her softly, a hand shaking her firmly.

Struggling to open her eyes, she fought against the blankets that had twisted themselves around her. Wrapped tightly against her body, she couldn't breathe. Fire surrounded her on all sides, and she screamed in terror when she couldn't break free.

"Candy!" Gary's voice cut through the nightmare, and her eyes shot open.

"Gary!" she screamed. "Oh my God, you're here!" She fought to sit up and threw her arms around his neck.

Perching on the edge of the couch, he held her. "I'm here, sweetness. Everything's ok." His words comforted her as he squeezed her tightly. "Fast response was our saving grace, and we didn't lose anyone that we know of," he informed her with his lips pressed against her hair. "Everyone's safe."

Her body shook as she sobbed against his broad chest, breathing in the scent of him. "I thought I had lost you. That I would never see you again. I wanted to believe that you would be fine, but I couldn't," she bellowed.

"Shh," he soothed, stroking her back firmly. "It's ok, baby. I'm home, and I'm safe."

At that moment, Gary knew he would never work in the field again. Candy couldn't take it even as badly as she wanted to. She had lost too much and feared too much, and he could never ask that of her, to live with knowing that one day he might not come home. He had never considered his mother's offer, but that night, he knew his days as a fireman, even an investigator, were numbered.

Allowing her to cry, he held her until her tears were spent. Then pushing against her, he helped her to sit up properly. "You did a good job on the house," he praised, smoothing her hair out of her face. "Everything looks well managed. I'm proud of you."

"I didn't go start the generator," she confessed. "I figured it could wait until morning if we still need it."

"Yeah, I'll go at first light if we're still without power. For now, this is fine. We have heat, and everyone else is asleep," he agreed.

Pushing her over, he burrowed into the corner next to her. He breathed deeply, holding her firmly against him with his left arm, and his right toying with her hand. Her special hand. His digits traced her finger where he would soon place his ring. "Candy?" he whispered, unsure if she had fallen back to sleep.

"Yes?" she replied in a sluggish tone.

"I love you, Candice Parker. I don't care if this blizzard postpones everything. I'm going to marry you. Don't you ever doubt it."

Smiling, she nestled deeper against him, entwining her fingers with his. "I know you are, Mr. Ford. And I have to say I'm fairly looking forward to it."

"Fairly?" He chuckled, kissing the top of her head. "We're going to have a good life, kitten. I promise you that." Listening to her breathe, he could tell she was exhausted and let her drift off to sleep now that she could dream in peace.

Five days of frigid cold blanketed the state, and the four of them spent that time reading, playing, and talking in quiet chats. They ran the generator in the mornings and evenings, and the fire kept them warm during the night. On the day that should have been their ceremony, Candy could feel the ache in her chest.

"Well, I guess we're officially postponed," she sighed over breakfast.

"Postponed but not canceled." Gary grinned, wishing they had consummated their relationship sooner and he could have spent this time making love to her. "It will come. We have to be patient."

Taking his hand, she agreed, "Yes, but it may just be the four of us and the judge at this point. Do you think we should wait until next week even if the snow clears?" The thought made her feel forlorn, as she had grown tired of waiting, had wanted the day to be special despite everything seeming stacked against it.

"I think we'll play it by ear," he suggested, kissing her fingers lightly. "We planned a small, simple ceremony, so at least we can be thankful for that."

The pair of them jumped when the phone rang. "I guess at least land service has been restored," he observed as he stood to answer it. Discovering his mother on the other end, he grinned broadly as he listened.

Unable to discern what she wanted, Candy picked at her fingers and waited. When he finally stated, "Ok, Mom. I promise," before he hung up, she heaved a small sigh.

"That didn't sound good," she moped as he reclaimed his seat beside her.

"Oh, it's not bad," he reassured. "She wants to make sure we don't hold the wedding without them." He beamed.

"You're kidding!" Candy gasped. "I thought she hated me."

"Well, I can't speak on that part, but I know she has a surprise for you—one that she says must be delivered before the ceremony. As soon as we get things set, we'll let them know, and she can bring it with them," he planned aloud. "And now that I think of it, I also have a surprise for you."

Eyeing her fiancé warily, a slow grin covered her

face. Her mind racing over all the crazy things he could have in mind, she gave in. "Ok, what is it?"

"I had lunch with Mom the other day," he confessed. "One of the vice presidents of the company will be retiring after the first of the year."

"And?" Her heart pounded, unsure where this was leading.

"And I'm going to take the job. She's been harassing me for years to get on board, and I think this would be a good time." He smiled, hoping the news would please her.

On the contrary, Candy appeared stunned. "Gary, you love your job!"

"Yeah, I know." He opened a palm to the ceiling in a half shrug. "But I love you more. I know you worry about me, and I took the desk job so you wouldn't have to worry. The blizzard only served to prove that I didn't get far enough away from it."

"You really mean that?" she asked airily. "I would never ask you to change who you are." Her eyes grew misty. "I'm really sorry that I've upset you."

"Oh, baby." He pulled her against him. "You haven't upset me. You've made things clearer for me. What's important in my life…and my future."

Running her hand over his chest, she could feel the beat of his heart beneath his shirt. "I guess that's true for both of us," she agreed, then had a wild thought. "Hey!" She sat up to stare at him. "Do you think they will have any openings after I finish school, in your family's company?"

"You want to work for us?" he chortled, picturing his mother as her boss.

"Yeah, well, maybe! What exactly do they do?" She grinned.

"Oh, Candy." He hugged her back to his chest. "Such a silly girl. I love my Christmas Candy."

FOURTEEN

Truth and Lies

TIME EKED BY, or so it seemed, cooped up in the house with a six-year-old. By the twenty-second, much of the city was back to normal, or close to it, just in time for the holiday. When the electricity came back on, they knew things had reached a turning point, and Gary set to work making the calls to get everyone gathered, starting with the judge.

A friendly old man, he agreed to come the following evening to perform the ceremony, to which the couple eagerly agreed. Texting her few friends, Candy felt relieved that the cell and cable service had come back online as well and used her computer to check her grades: four As and one B.

Well, not a bad start, but next semester it's going to be all As, she promised herself earnestly. Making a post on her Facebook page, she announced that the ceremony was on for anyone else who might be interested in knowing, and it gave her an odd feeling of joy to think that anyone else might care what was going on in her life.

Bouncing down the stairs a few minutes later, she announced, "We have to figure out where everyone is sleeping tonight."

"In their beds, don't you think?" Gary chuckled.

"No, silly. I mean so that we can get up tomorrow without seeing each other," she informed him with her hands on her hips.

"Oh, I forgot." He continued to grin. "You believe it will be bad luck if we do."

"Yes, it will, and that means you have to get out of the house before I come down. I presume that you are going to work tomorrow."

"Yes," he agreed more somberly. "I'll be handing in my resignation," he announced to the rest of the family.

"Are you sure?" Lanelle appeared somewhat dismayed at the news.

"Afraid so." He scooped up Daks and gave him a playful shake. "Going to take a job with my family's company in January. About time, I guess."

"Oh, that's wonderful news!" She clasped her hands together joyfully. "Well, don't worry about tomorrow. I'll let Candice know when you are safely out of the house, and she'll be in her room getting ready when you get home. And you can get dressed in my room."

"We'll be getting ready in your room," Candy informed her. "You're walking me down the aisle, remember? You have to get dressed too!"

"I'll be ready before he gets home. No worries." Lanelle beamed. "That way I can play hostess as your guests arrive. How many will we be having again?"

"Looks like less than twenty," Gary cut in. "Bobby and Carl will be over tomorrow with the chairs, and they'll take care of rearranging the living room and setting everything up. Candy sketched it for us, and it looks as if everything is going to fit great. All you have to do is take care of the refreshments in the dining room and we're all set." He indicated Candy with a small nod.

"Sounds like a plan." She smoothed her shirt and stood up straighter. "I'll take care of it before I change." A swarm of butterflies took flight in her belly. "Oh my God. This is really happening. We're getting married tomorrow!"

"You bet we are." He pulled her into his arms, her head against his chest as he hugged her forcefully before he bent over to kiss her. "This is the last time I will kiss you as my fiancée, for tomorrow you will be my wife."

"Can't wait." She giggled, running her palm over the stubble on his cheek. Giving him another peck on the lips, she turned and dashed up the stairs.

The following morning, things went off without a hitch, and Gary had already left by the time Candy poured her cup of coffee. At noon, his cousins showed up with a truckload of chairs and rearranged the living room by moving one of the couches to the den. Setting up the seats in the expanded space, everything was in place and ready to go.

Helping her mother make the punch, Candy also added a few bottles of wine to the fridge. They had never been big on it at her house, especially since her mother's bout with alcoholism. But Gary's family seemed to live on the stuff, which brought a small smile to her lips knowing they would soon be her family, too.

Once everything was set, she made one last check on Dakota, who played quietly in the den, and then made her way upstairs. Anxious tingles of electric excitement danced through her body as Candy applied her makeup and set her hair in rollers. Finally, she pulled down her lacey dress and slipped it on. Glancing at the clock, she would be ready with only half an hour to spare.

"That's good though," she mumbled to herself. "Less time to be nervous."

"Nervous about what? Marrying my son?" Eve announced her presence with a flourish.

"Oh, Eveline," Candy gasped. "You startled me."

"Apparently so." The older woman stepped forward, pulling the shorter girl in for a hug. "I'm so happy for you, Candy. For you and Dakota and for my son." Her smile appeared genuine, and the girl eyed her warily.

Not waiting to give an explanation, Eve pushed on. "Candy, I met an old friend of yours the other day. We got to talk and had a very illuminating discussion. Dakota's father doesn't think very highly of you." She paused, watching the girl's face. "But we do. Today, Daks will become my grandson, and you will be my daughter. I am truly pleased by that."

Handing the girl the folded agreement, she smiled. "Have a happy life, Candice. You bring joy to my son, and I could never ask for any more than that."

Unfolding the page with trembling digits, Candy could feel the tears threatening to ruin her makeup before she could even make it down the stairs. Beginning at the top, she read the page, her lips moving as she took in each word and phrase. "What does this mean?" she demanded when she reached the bottom.

"You have to sign it." Eveline offered her a pen. "It's an agreement between you, me, and Cliff. I will pay him two hundred and fifty thousand dollars, and he will sign away his rights to Dakota. And if or when Gary is ready, he can adopt him."

Candy stared at her in disbelief. "You would do that for me? For us? That's an awful lot of money!" As soon as the words had been spoken, a much sadder thought occurred to her. "He never intended to be a part of Dakota's life, did he? This was his plan all along, wasn't it? He lied to me."

"Truth and lies are seldom black and white." Eve lifted her chin. "This is what is best for your son, for your family, and it will be a small price to pay in my estimation."

"I see." Candy refolded the page. "Well, in that case, I won't sign it."

A look of fear mixed with anger crossed the older woman's features. "What do you mean, won't sign it?"

"I mean this isn't right. You can still give him the money, and he can disappear if he wants. Someday, Gary may even adopt him. But Dakota deserves to have that person in his corner. The chance that one day his father will be a part of his life…whenever he's ready," Candy quietly explained. She had made peace with the situation, and she hoped that her new mother-in-law would agree and see things as she did.

"Candy, I really don't understand," Eveline's voice quavered.

"I know that Gary loves Daks." The young woman smoothed her dress as she attempted to make her decision clear. "And he will be a good dad. But I don't want to close that door forever. Cliff's still pretty young, and as he gets older, he may realize what he's missed out on, not being a part of Dakota's life. That's what matters to me. And then Daks will have two dads. How lucky could one boy be?" She grinned through her tears and then reached out her arms in offer of a hug.

Accepting the gesture, Eve gave her a squeeze. "You are a beautiful person, Candice. Inside and out." Stepping back a moment later, she glanced at her watch. "It's time to go down," she informed her. "Your mother is waiting to give you away."

FIFTEEN

Christmas Eve

GARY STOOD in front of the fireplace, anxiously locking and unlocking his knees. Everything in place, every seat taken, a few chairs had been added from the dining room to accommodate everyone. *Just breathe,* he reminded himself sternly. Watching the stairs, he could see his mother descend and a flutter of activity as Lanelle moved to await her daughter's arrival.

"Hello, gorgeous," he whispered to himself when she came into view, his mind spiraling back to the nights he had visited her at the convenience store. The very sight of her still took his breath away.

Dimly aware of music, he watched Lanelle holding Candy's arm as they stepped in rhythm towards him. She had called her dress sensible, but the only word he could think of was stunning. Her honey brown hair swept back and topped with a ring of cream-colored roses, she had never been more radiant.

Taking her hand when she joined him, the couple turned to face the judge. He could hear the words and did his best to stammer through when instructed to "repeat after me," but his pulse beat too loudly in his ears for any of it to make sense. Then, hearing Candy's sweet voice as she spoke, his heart slowed and felt calmer, as if her very existence had soothed his chaotic being.

A moment later, he lifted the veil to find the clearest pair of hazel eyes he had ever seen staring up at him. She was taller in her heels, but he leaned forward to close the remaining gap. Her lips warm and soft beneath his, his chest ached, with everything moving in slow motion before it exploded into hyper speed, and the next thing he knew, it was over.

Standing in place next to the modest cake that had been chosen, Gary grinned down at the tiny plastic couple. "See. I knew it wasn't flowers on top," he pointed out with a laugh.

"Yeah, well," Candy shot back, her smile broad as they cut the cake and then posed for pictures.

Eventually, the photographer had enough, and they could mingle and enjoy their guests. Looking around anxiously, Candy found her son crashed in the den, along with the rest of the children watching a movie. Standing in the doorway observing him, she felt a joy so pure she thought it might consume her.

Sliding his arm around from behind, Gary whispered in her ear, "Don't worry. He's safe."

"I know." She inhaled deeply, preparing to tell him what had transpired with Dakota's father. "I need to talk to you when this is over." She turned to face him. "Your mother's been busy, and I think you need to know what she did."

Standing straighter, his brow furrowed, he replied, "You mean about Cliff."

"Yes." She appeared surprised. "How did you know?"

"Dad told me after she went up to see you. I guess it's done then." He lifted her hand to kiss it, massaging her fingers gently.

"No, it isn't done." She leaned against the door frame as if all her energy had been drained. "I appreciate her generosity, but I'm afraid that I can't close that door completely. I'll support you if you decide to adopt Daks, but I never want to see Cliff stripped of his rights even if he never chooses to act on them. Some day he may want to, and I owe him that much, I think."

Nodding, Gary caressed her cheek. "I understand. We'll leave it open then. With Mother's payment, he'll leave us alone and can't ever try to take him again. But if he decides to visit, he will have the option."

"Yes," Candy breathed in relief. "I'm so glad you understand."

His eyes dancing, Gary shook his head slowly.

"Men aren't as complicated as you think we are. We're quite simple, in fact. Don't mess with our women or our children and things run pretty smoothly."

"Is that so?" She stretched up in an attempt to kiss him.

Lowering his mouth to hers, he obliged, enjoying the sweet taste of her. "So now what, Mrs. Ford?"

"Mrs. Ford is your mother," she giggled back.

"Well, then I guess that's two things you have in common," he toyed with her.

"Two things? What's the first?"

"You are both very special to me." His eyes wrinkled when he grinned. "You have to admit she did come to your rescue. Pretty thoughtful, don't you think? Almost like a special Christmas gift."

"Yeah, a really expensive one," Candy agreed. "That is funny though when you think about it."

"What is?" he replied, appearing lost in being close to her.

"Well, you're always calling me your Christmas Candy." She chuckled. "And so I guess your mother is your Christmas Eve."

Gary dropped his head back and laughed out loud. "That's true," he confessed jovially. "I've always loved this time of year. And with you in my life, I think it's just going to keep getting better and better."

"It will if I have any say in the matter. Now, when do we get to run these people out of here? It's going to be bedtime soon," she purred.

"Oh, you bet it is." He kissed her again. "And I've got some promises to keep," he stated firmly before swinging around to begin bidding everyone a good night.

Thank You

Thank you for reading, and I hope that you have enjoyed the 2016 installment of the Sweet Christmas Series. Look for a new adventure for Gary and Candy at Christmas next year. ~ Sam

Books in this series include:
    Christmas Candy (2015)
    Christmas Eve (2016)
    Christmas Carol (2017)
    Christmas Joy (2018)
    Christmas Holly (2019)
    Christmas Lane (2020)

About the Author

Anyone who knows me could tell you, I am a friendly kind of person, never met a stranger and take up conversations anywhere at any time. I work hard, and my mind never seems to shut down, as I wake up often in the middle of the night with ideas pouring out and demanding to be dealt with. Of course that means much of my books were written in the middle of the night.

I grew up and still live in the great state of Texas where everything is bigger, where we have warm weather and a central location. I love my state, my town, and my family, which includes my four sons, my significant other, and many friends as well.

I have thoroughly enjoyed writing this story and hope that you will love reading it just as much. And of course, there will be many more adventures to come.

You can follow Samantha Jacobey at:

Facebook: https://www.facebook.com/SamJacobey
Twitter: https://twitter.com/SamJacobey
Pinterest: http://www.pinterest.com/samanthajacobey/

Also by SAMANTHA JACOBEY

http://www.amazon.com/-/e/B00GEB5LX0

A New Life Series – an epic adventure, TORI FARRELL's life IS one wild story... escaped from a biker gang and running from drug lords... used by the FBI and hoping to protect her present from her past... IT'S DARK - IT'S BRUTAL, and it's WORTH EVERY MINUTE OF IT!! (Mature read, 18+ for graphic sexual content and violence, including rape)

Summer Spirit Novella Series - no one EVER had a summer romance like this... Charlie visits another plane, parallel to our own, where Summer Angels and Dark Angels battle over the fate of man. A unique twist on an old idea that will keep you guessing; will Charlie and Clarisse ever find their HEA? (New adult)

Teach Me to Prey – in this standalone thriller, JASON TRUITT and his friends have gotten their way for years. Deceit, sex, and foul play aren't normally covered in the curriculum, but they're doing whatever it takes to get under BECKY STEWART's skin. When one of the boys turns up dead, it's a race against time to save the others; a STUNNING STORY that will get your heart racing and leave you breathless by the end... (New Adult)

The Binding (Unexpected Magic #1) - One cursed diary will change two strangers forever...Can Meri and Rider use her mother's old book to figure out why someone is after them? Or will the guilty party succeed, ripping the tome away before killing them and then slithering back into the darkness… (New Adult)

The Wicked Awakened (Unexpected Magic #2) – a Halloween novel; a five-hundred-year-old witch wants to turn SARAH MATTHEWS' body into her new home… A twisted tale involving a coven hell bent on seeing that she succeeds. Who will come out on top in this epic battle of wills? (Mature read, 18+ for graphic sexual content and violence)

The Irrevocable Series - From affluent beginnings, BAILEY DEWITT's life has become a broken mess... after her parents died unexpectedly, she didn't think it could get any worse. But when the arrogance of man catches up and puts the entire world into a dooms-day spiral, there will be only ONE PLACE she can run to - the ONE PLACE she wanted desperately to escape. (New Adult)

The Dragon of Eriden Series - Amicia Spicer led a simple life, until she discovered it had all been a lie… On her deathbed, Arely Spicer confessed to her only daughter that she had been found by, not born to her mother and father. Sad news to be certain, the idea of having a family of flesh and blood waiting to be reunited sent the young, independent woman on the adventure of a lifetime. Little did she know, a dragon's heart beat within her chest and her journey would be more perilous than she could have imagined... (New Adult)

Also from our Lavish family

Love on the Double Duo
By L.A. Remenicky
http://mybook.to/LoveOnTheDoubleDuo

The Monroe brothers fall fast, they fall hard, and they fall forever. But the road to true love isn't always easy.

Loving Jessie's Girl – Book 1: Until AJ Monroe left Indiana after college he had always lived in his identical twin brother's shadow. He had made a life for himself in Denver, Colorado, away from Jessie, away from Indiana. But when AJ feared for his brother's safety, he left everything behind to step back into the shadow he thought he had outgrown. Finding his brother was AJ's only concern...until he met Jessie's girl.

Fiercely independent, Rina Abbot hid her true situation from everyone, including her best friend, Jessie. Out of money and unable to care for her rescue dogs she had no choice but to accept the help of the handsome stranger with a familiar face. Afraid to trust him, she tried to ignore the feelings he stirred within her as they searched for his missing brother.

But secrets never stay secrets for long.

Finally open about their feelings for each other, Rina's secrets began to wreak havoc on their lives. Would Rina's secrets force AJ to give up his dream of loving Jessie's girl?

Beyond Duty – Book 2: After serving in the Marine Corps, Jessie Monroe has finally found a life beyond war. He's focused on being an EMT and helping his best friend rescue dogs, until he happens upon a curvy blonde stranded with a flat tire and no jack.

On the run from her past, Dori Graham is slow to trust any man, and she tries to ignore the spark of interest she feels for her handsome savior, but a friendship grows between them.

When Dori's past invades her new life, Jessie vows to rescue her. Saving her will take him beyond duty and into his own personal hell. Calling upon his training as a Marine and the depth of his feelings for

Dori, Jessie will need the mental strength to battle to save her and, ultimately, save himself.

Also from our Lavish family

Between the Trees
Kathy Moczerniak
http://mybook.to/betweenthetrees

A beautiful coming of age with a dark side that one teenager must fight to overcome…

Beyond Kathryn Lucas' first memory of her father's tree lay a dysfunctional path of violence, heartbreak, and secrets within a family severely entrenched in the vicious cycle of abuse. A lifetime of fear drives her from her home, and the teenage girl finds refuge with an aunt and uncle determined to protect their niece.

Distressing flashbacks unravel in Kathryn's fragile mind among the turmoil encircling her as she struggles through adolescence and descends into her pain-ridden past. When the summation of her unsettling memories allows the darkness to overtake her, she becomes desperate to unearth the light.

Inspired by a true story, Kathryn must hold on tightly to those who love her, searching for her place in a world threatening to break her as she fights to overcome life's betrayals before she is deprived of her future.

The Hunter Series
Sara J. Bernhardt
http://mybook.to/HuntersTril

Jane Callahan is a reclusive, seventeen-year-old high school student dealing with the death of her beloved brother. Her home in Southern California with her mother is a constant reminder of her loss and pain. In hopes of escaping her past she moves to North Bend Oregon to live with her father, where she meets a beautiful boy named Aidan Summers.

Jane is intrigued by his looks as well as his unusual ways of attempting to get her attention. After months of uncommon conversation and frustration, an uncertain romance brews between Jane and Aidan, but Aidan has a ghastly secret that could destroy everything.

www.ingramcontent.com/pod-product-compliance
Lightning Source LLC
Chambersburg PA
CBHW051300170626
46809CB00004B/1737